CHECKPOINTS IN THIS BOOK ✔

WORD COUNT	GUIDED READING LEVEL	NUMBER OF DOLCH SIGHT WORDS
722	G	94

READING TOGETHER

READING OUT LOUD

READING INDEPENDENTLY

READY TO READ MORE

WELCOME TO
PASSPORT TO READING
A beginning reader's ticket to a brand-new world!

Every book in this program is designed to build read-along and read-alone skills, level by level, through engaging and enriching stories. As the reader turns each page, he or she will become more confident with new vocabulary, sight words, and comprehension.

These PASSPORT TO READING levels will help you choose the perfect book for every reader.

READING TOGETHER
Read short words in simple sentence structures together to begin a reader's journey.

READING OUT LOUD
Encourage developing readers to sound out words in more complex stories with simple vocabulary.

READING INDEPENDENTLY
Newly independent readers gain confidence reading more complex sentences with higher word counts.

READY TO READ MORE
Readers prepare for chapter books with fewer illustrations and longer paragraphs.

This book features sight words from the educator-supported Dolch Sight Words List. This encourages the reader to recognize commonly used vocabulary words, increasing reading speed and fluency.

For more information, please visit passporttoreadingbooks.com.

Enjoy the journey!

Little, Brown and Company

Hachette Book Group
237 Park Avenue, New York, NY 10017
Visit our website at lb-kids.com

Little, Brown and Company is a division of Hachette Book Group, Inc. The Little, Brown name and logo are trademarks of Hachette Book Group, Inc.

The publisher is not responsible for websites (or their content) that are not owned by the publisher.

First Edition: February 2014
Originally published in 2011 by HarperCollins Publishers

Library of Congress Control Number: 2013950707

ISBN 978-0-316-32486-1

10 9 8 7 6 5 4 3 2 1

WOR

Printed in the United States of America

Passport to Reading titles are leveled by independent reviewers applying the standards developed by Irene Fountas and Gay Su Pinnell in *Matching Books to Readers: Using Leveled Books in Guided Reading*, Heinemann, 1999.

Licensed By:

MY LITTLE PONY

PHONICS FUN

by Joanne Mattern

LITTLE, BROWN AND COMPANY
New York • Boston

Table of Contents

PONY FRIENDS
INTRODUCTION

In this story you will learn new sight words.
Can you find these words?

a

all

I

is

like

my

we

Here are some fun My Little Pony words:

friends

meet

name

pink

pony

Hello!

My name is Twilight Sparkle.

Let's meet some of my pony friends.

This is Applejack.

I like Applejack.

Applejack

Hello, Rarity!

Rarity is my friend.

Here is a pony friend.

She is Fluttershy!

Hello, Fluttershy!

Here is a pink pony.

I like pink ponies!

This pony is Pinkie Pie.

I like my pony friends.

And we all like you!

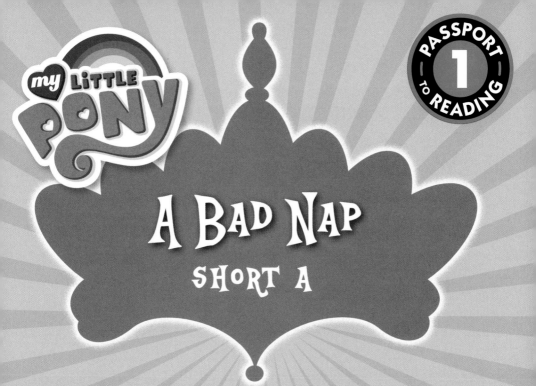

A Bad Nap

SHORT A

In this story you will learn
about the **short a** vowel sound.
Can you find these words and sound them out?

bad

can

had

nap

ran

Here are some fun My Little Pony words:

away   dream   sleepy

Here are some new sight words:

go	saw
make	she
said	the

Pinkie Pie was sleepy.

Pinkie Pie took a nap.

Pinkie Pie had a bad dream.

She saw a bad monster.

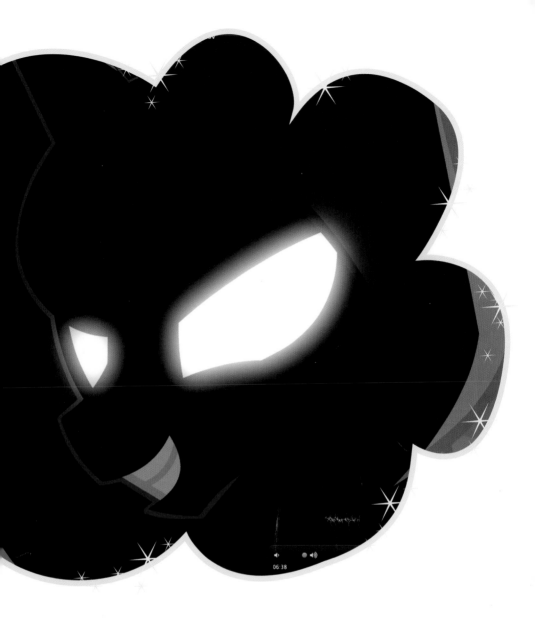

06:38

Pinkie Pie ran.

She ran away from the bad monster.

"I can help!" Rainbow Dash said.

Rainbow Dash woke her friend.

Pinkie Pie told her friend her bad dream.

"Friends can make bad dreams go away!"
said Rainbow Dash.

GET SET FOR FUN
SHORT E

In this story you will learn
about the **short e** vowel sound.
Can you find these words and sound them out?

dresses

let's

pets

ten

tents

went

Here are some fun My Little Pony words:

outside   pretty   treats

Here are some new sight words:

play

to

they

what

"Let's play," said Rainbow Dash.

"Let's play outside."

"Let's play with pets!" said Fluttershy.
She likes to play with pets.

48

"Now let's play dress-up!" said Rarity.

She and her friends put on pretty dresses.

Later, the ponies set up small tents.

Then they ate ten treats.

"What a fun day!" said the ponies.

And then they all went home.

Bad Luck, Good Luck

Short U

In this story you will learn
about the **short u** vowel sound.
Can you find these words and sound them out?

but

fun

luck

sun

up

Here are some fun My Little Pony words:

balloons

fly

kite

Here are some new sight words:

look

that

The ponies are flying kites!

Twilight Sparkle has a kite.

Look at that!

Up goes the kite.

It goes up to the sun!

Twilight Sparkle gets her kite.

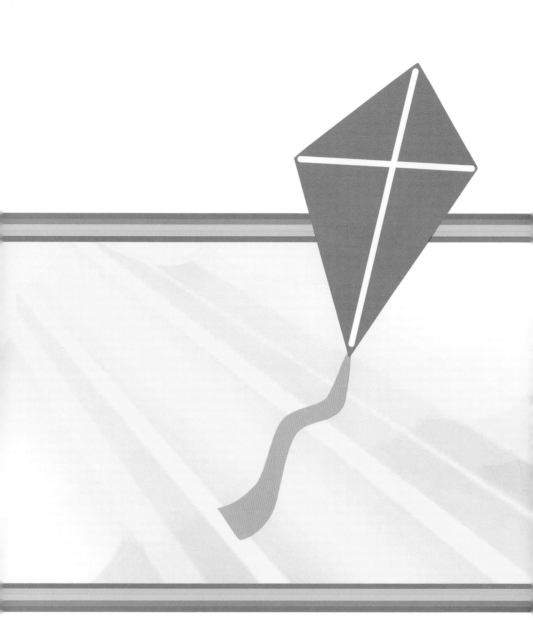

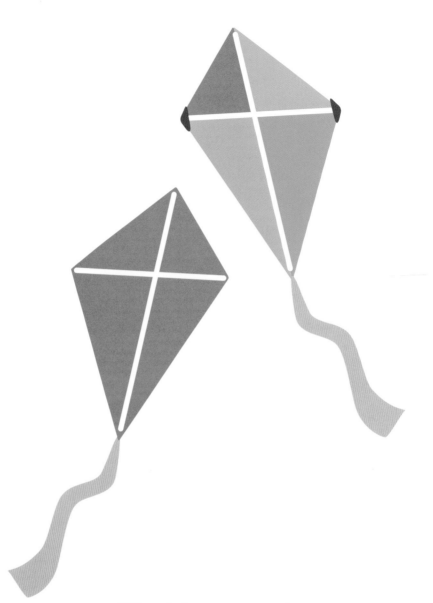

The kites go up!

This is fun!

Bad luck!

The kites fly away.

Look at the balloons!

The balloons go up to the sun.

This is fun!

Bad luck!

The balloons fly away.

"Kites and balloons fly up and away," said Twilight Sparkle. "But friends are forever!"

PASSPORT TO READING 1

THE BIG FAIR

SHORT i

In this story you will learn
about the **short i** vowel sound.
Can you find these words and sound them out?

big

hill

hit

kicked

pick

skipped

slid

win

Here are some fun My Little Pony words:

fair

prize

Here are some new sight words:

do

down

The ponies skipped down the road.

They skipped to the big fair.

73

"Let's pick a fun thing to do," said Rainbow Dash.

The ponies slid.

They slid down a hill.

They slid down fast!

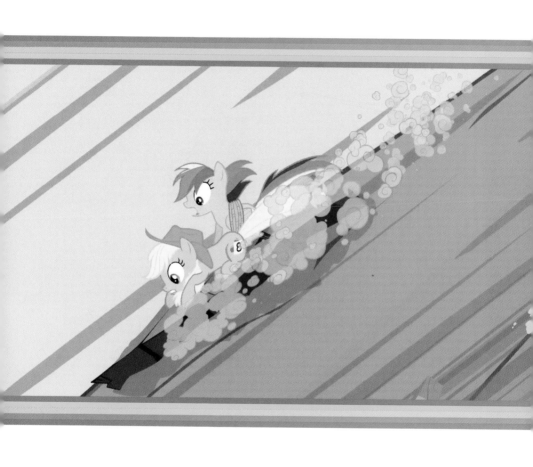

Rainbow Dash picked a game.

She kicked a ball.

"I win!" Rainbow Dash said.

Rainbow Dash picked a prize.

The big fair was a big hit!

THE HOT DAY
SHORT O

In this story you will learn
about the **short o** vowel sound.
Can you find these words and sound them out?

hot

lots

pop

stopped

Here are some fun My Little Pony words:

beach

hello

sand

Here are some new sight words:

are

of

very

It was hot.

It was a very hot day.

The ponies were at the beach.

The sand was hot!

"I have an ice pop," said Rainbow Dash.

"I like ice pops on hot days!"

Pinkie Pie went in the water.

She had fun.

Fluttershy stopped to say hello.

95

"Hot days are lots of fun!" said Pinkie Pie.

Pinkie Pie's Band

Short A

In this story you will learn
about the **short** a vowel sound.
Do you remember these words?

can   had

Can you find these words and sound them out?

band

clapped

glad

plan

sad

Here are some fun My Little Pony words:

sang   sing   song   start

Here are some new sight words:

be

don't

wanted

was

Pinkie Pie had a plan.

She wanted to start a band.

The ponies were glad.

They liked Pinkie Pie's plan.

103

Rainbow Dash and Fluttershy sang.

They sang a song.

Pinkie Pie was sad.

She wanted to sing a song.

"Don't be sad," said the ponies.

"All of us can sing a song."

Pinkie Pie was glad.

Everyone clapped for the band.

A New Friend

SHORT E

In this story you will learn
about the **short e** vowel sound.
Do you remember this word?

went

Can you find these words and sound them out?

bent

best

fed

pet

spend

Here are some fun My Little Pony words:

found friend

Here are some new sight words:

her

say

with

Fluttershy went outside.

She found her pony friends.

"Let's spend the day outside!" they said.

The ponies went for a walk.

"Look!

A new friend!" said Twilight Sparkle.

"Let's pet the rabbit!" said Fluttershy.
She bent down to say hello.

Then Fluttershy went home
with her new friend.
She fed the rabbit.

"New friends are the best!" said Fluttershy.

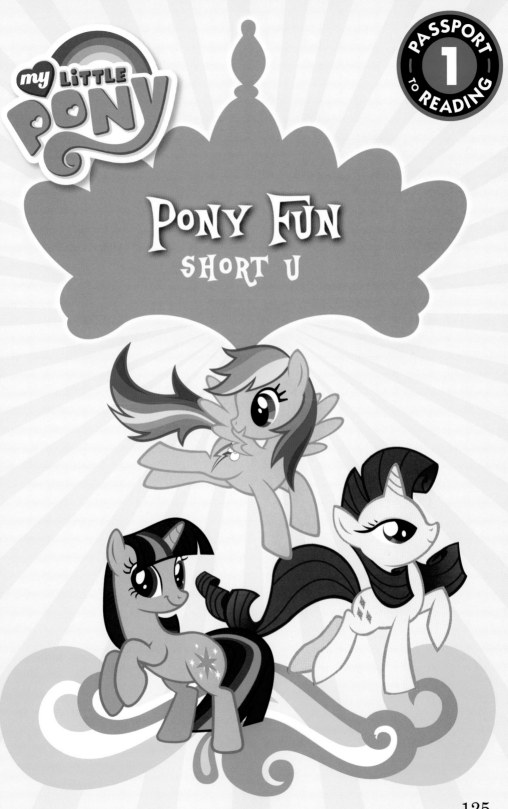

PONY FUN
SHORT U

In this story you will learn
about the **short u** vowel sound.
Do you remember these words?

fun

up

Can you find these words and sound them out?

hug

jumped

spun

umbrellas

Here are some fun My Little Pony words:

danced

nice

stage

Here is a new sight word:

loved

The ponies had fun.

The ponies played dress-up.

Rarity jumped up on the stage.

She loved her nice dress!

Twilight Sparkle and Pinkie Pie wore umbrellas.

The pony spun around.

The ponies got up.

They jumped and danced.

Then they all shared a big hug.

THE PONY PICNIC
SHORT i

In this story you will learn
about the **short** i vowel sound.
Do you remember this word?

big

hit

Can you find these words and sound them out?

dish

mixes

picks

picnic

will

Here are some fun My Little Pony words:

cupcakes

stirs

tasty

Here is a new sight word:

today

Today is a good day for a pony picnic.

Pinkie Pie will make a nice dish.

What will she make?

Pinkie Pie stirs.

Pinkie Pie mixes.

Pinkie Pie picks up the dish.

149

Pinkie Pie makes tasty cupcakes.

The pony picnic is a big hit!

A Letter from a Friend

SHORT O

In this story you will learn
about the **short o** vowel sound.
Do you remember this word?

not

Can you find these words and sound them out?

clock

got

lost

lots

mailbox

stop

Here are some fun My Little Pony words:

party

sleepover

Here are some new sight words:

brought

there

Every mailbox had a letter in it from Twilight Sparkle.

The letter said, "Come to my sleepover party!"

All the ponies got the letter.

"I must stop baking and take a nap," said Applejack.

"I have got to set the clock," said Applejack.

Then she took a nap.

There were lots of friends at the party.

But not Applejack.

Her clock had not rung.

But all was not lost.

The ponies brought the party

to Applejack's house!

PONY PARTY
REVIEW

In this story you will review the vowel sounds.
Can you find these words and sound them out?

and	jumped
best	lots
big	ran
fun	wish

Here are some fun My Little Pony words:

baked   cakes   party   pies   pony

Do you remember these sight words?

a	so
are	they
I	today
said	was
she	we

Today was a big day.

Today was the day of the pony party!

Pinkie Pie baked.

Pinkie Pie baked pies.

She baked lots of cakes.

Rainbow Dash made a wish.

"I wish for a fun party!"

The ponies played games.

They ran.

They jumped.

Then butterflies came.

"They are so pretty!" said Fluttershy.

179

"This was the best party!" said Pinkie Pie. "And we are best friends!"

DON'T MISS THESE OTHER PONY-RIFFIC BOOKS!

CHECK OUT THESE PONY-RIFFIC BOOKS, TOO!

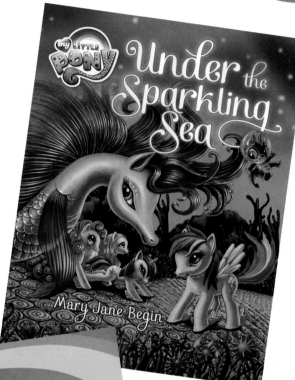

my LITTLE PONY

Under the Sparkling Sea

Mary Jane Begin

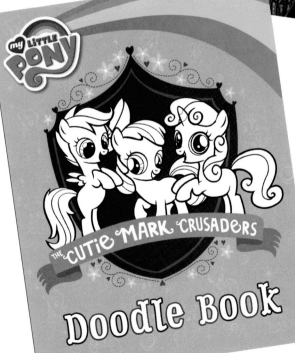

my LITTLE PONY

THE CUTIE MARK CRUSADERS

Doodle Book